Mycroft Holmes
& The Adventure of the Silver Birches

DAVID DICKINSON

First published 2011 by Endeavour Press Ltd.
This edition published by Sharpe Books in 2019.

Mycroft Holmes
& The Adventure of the Silver Birches

by David Dickinson

The rain started just after three o'clock. At first it was just a drizzle. As the minutes ticked past, it grew in force until it turned torrential by half past five as the workers of London began their journeys home. It poured off the sides of the buses. It hurtled down from the high buildings, overflowing from the gutters and sheeting down the walls and the windows. The prudent few raised their umbrellas but they gave little cover. The men with hats gained some protection but they soon felt the rain dripping down the backs of their collars. The bareheaded felt they were walking through a waterfall without end, a waterfall that bore them a grudge, a waterfall that wanted to turn them into bundles of soaked rags. Up Farringdon Road and Moorgate they trudged, along Poultry and London Wall on their way home to Islington and Hackney and places where the humbler people dwelt.

Among the sodden, soaking, dripping mass of humanity there was a policeman, Inspector Lestrade of Scotland Yard, returning to his villa at Brickfield Terrace in Upper Holloway. Inspector Lestrade's wife, Carrie, always referred to it as a villa when they were entertaining friends at home. Lestrade was not so sure. As he cursed the weather and waited for his bus, the Inspector was thinking of the meeting he had just left. It had been one of the most extraordinary meetings he had ever attended in his long professional career. It was held in the ornate offices of the Governor of the Bank of England in Threadneedle Street. Lestrade's own superior officer, the Commissioner of the Metropolitan Police was present, staring sadly at the carpet most of the time. Lestrade thought he would remember the conversation for the rest of his life.

"Good of you to come," said the Governor. "Pity about the weather. But nothing could be more serious than what we are here to consider this afternoon."

"Let me impress on you, Lestrade," the Commissioner was looking at him severely, as if he were a schoolboy found smoking behind the cricket pavilion, "you must not breathe a word of this to any living soul. Not to your wife, not to your best friend, not even to your mistress, if you have one, which I rather doubt. Not a word."

Lestrade turned a bright shade of red at the mention of the word mistress. Was the Commissioner not aware of his regular attendance at the Presbyterian Church in Upper Holloway? Did he not know that he, Lestrade, was an elder?

"What do you know about the currency, Lestrade?" the Governor was examining a large cigar as he spoke.

"The currency?" Lestrade was puzzled. This was something so secret he could not mention it and it had to do with currency? "Pound notes? Coins? That sort of thing?" he ventured.

"Pound notes are what concern us here. Notes of every denomination. Pound notes and their universal acceptance are one of the foundation stones of this great economy of ours, Lestrade. Without that confidence underpinning every financial transaction, we would be lost."

Lestrade wondered if he had wandered into an evening class by mistake. Whatever might be coming next?

"We are convinced, here at the Bank," the Governor had lowered his voice till he was virtually whispering, "that our enemies are trying to debase the currency."

Now he leant back in his chair as if he were a magician who has finally pulled the rabbit out of his hat.

"Forgive me, Governor, I am just a simple policeman. I solve simple crimes. I know little of finance."

"Debasing the currency is quite simple once you have grasped the basics." The Commissioner of the Metropolitan Police had entered the lists at last. "Debasing the currency means lowering it in value. If you introduce enough forgeries into the system, the value of the pound will fall. Where once you paid for your groceries with a note from your wallet, after the lowering or debasing you might need a bucketful of notes. The result of debasing the currency is inflation. The value of the pound goes down, the prices in the shops are inflated, they're blown up like balloons, they go higher and higher."

"So how are our enemies doing this debasing?" Lestrade felt that a couple of grisly murders in Shadwell might be preferable to this.

"They're doing it through forged banknotes, that's what they're doing," said the Governor. "More and more are being introduced every week. We don't know how it's done or who the villains are. That is where you come in, Lestrade. You've got to find the forgers and the mastermind behind them. He must be the most dangerous man in

Europe."

"What are the sources for your information, Governor? Surely they could tell you who the forgers are and where they operate from."

"There is little I can say on that subject. All I can tell you is that we have three reliable sources – a private bank in Vienna, an Anglophile moneylender in Munich, an anonymous tip off from the Casino in Monte Carlo."

"Would I be permitted to go and see these gentlemen?" asked Lestrade.

"Certainly not," replied the Governor of the Bank of England. "Before you go, could I just say that our experts at present have great difficulty deciding which notes are the forgeries and which are the real thing. There is only one machine in the land that can help and it is kept under armed guard in the basement of the bank here. I know that doesn't help you much but it's the truth."

It was still raining hard when Lestrade arrived home. He was preoccupied during supper, eating his lamb chops as if he wasn't really there. What he found most difficult, as he wondered where to start his investigation, was deciding why he had been chosen. His friend and colleague Inspector Gregson would have been much more suitable.

Everybody said Gregson was clever. Nobody ever said Lestrade was clever. Dogged, people said. Determined. A British bulldog. But not clever. As he thought of where he might find help, Lestrade regretted yet again the departure from London of that extraordinary consulting detective, Sherlock Holmes, with whom he had co-operated on a number of difficult cases in the past. But Holmes had gone to keep bees in Sussex. Lestrade had an address for him. He had written to him before, he would write again before he retired for the night, but Holmes never replied to any correspondence. Only last Christmas he, Lestrade, had been sent a small monograph, privately printed, entitled 'Practical Handbook of Bee Culture, with some Observations upon the Segregation of the Queen.' And on the title page an ironic message. 'Alone I did it. Behold the fruit of pensive nights and laborious days, when I watched the little working gangs as once I watched the criminal world of London.' And Sherlock Holmes's great friend Dr Watson had returned to his medical practice. There was no-one outside the force he could turn to. It was only after supper, taking his customary glass of port with his pipe that inspiration came to Lestrade. He slapped his hand on his thigh and exclaimed.

"Mycroft! Of course! Mycroft Holmes, Sherlock's elder brother!"

"What was that, dear?" Carrie Lestrade looked up from her knitting.

"Nothing, dear, nothing. I was day dreaming, that's all."

"Inspector Lestrade! How nice to see you!"

Mrs Hudson, who had been Holmes and Watson's housekeeper at 221B Baker Street, had come to look after Mycroft Holmes in his rooms on Pall Mall.

"And you, Mrs Hudson? Keeping well are you?"

"I can't complain, Inspector. Mr Sherlock sends me a pot of honey on my birthday every year! Mr Mycroft got your note, he's waiting for you."

"Lestrade," the bulky figure of Mycroft Holmes rose slowly from his chair and shook him by the hand. "I'm glad to see you have recovered from the gout, Inspector. And I observe that you have recently finished painting the walls and ceilings of your house and transferred your weekend attentions to your garden."

"How on earth," Lestrade began, but Mycroft cut him short.

"My dear Lestrade, we have no time for idle gossip. Suffice it to say that when a man has gout he puts as much weight as he can on the heel of his shoe or boot, to ease the pressure and pain on his toe. The heel of your right boot is more worn than the left. So I deduce you have been treading heavily to assuage the pain of the gout. There is a faint hint of white paint in your hair above your left temple and a small sliver of earth under the nail of the index finger of your right hand. Really, my brother and I have always been astonished that other people seem unable or incapable of making these elementary deductions. However, to work. You mentioned forgery in your note. Pray tell me all you know of this matter."

Mycroft Holmes was seven years older than his brother Sherlock. The few who knew them both said that it was Mycroft who had the greater intellectual powers. Where Sherlock was thin, Mycroft was plump. His waistcoat, Lestrade observed, was a couple of sizes larger than it had been at their last meeting. He was taller than his brother, an imposing six feet three inches. And he had contracted psoriasis. Psoriasis appears as raised red patches of skin covered with silvery scales, sometimes on the head and neck, sometimes as red blotches all over the body. Dr Watson always described it as the itch and scratch disease. Every now and then Mycroft would rub the side of his scalp or his neck and a small cloud of white flakes would land on his shoulders. If he forgot to brush them off, as he often did, he began to resemble a man caught in a minor snowstorm, the flakes piling up in drifts.

Officially Mycroft's position inside the Government machine was that of an auditor. Over the years his role had been expanded until he had an oversight and an overview of all departments of state. As his brother put it, he was the one man capable of seeing how different areas of policy would interact, so that he was, from time to time, the British Government. He listened quietly to what Lestrade had to say.

"They have trouble telling the difference between the fakes and the real thing," he said sadly when the Governor's closing remarks were relayed to him. "There have been whispers about this, mind you, just whispers, one from New York last autumn and a hint, a scintilla of a murmur from Frankfurt this Easter. But it never came to anything." Mycroft formed his hands into a steeple, fingertips touching at the top and stared out at Pall Mall beyond his windows. His eyes, which were of a peculiarly light, watery grey, had a far-away, introspective look as if he was exerting his full powers. He thought for a couple of minutes, scratching his head a couple of times.

"That's it! That's it!" he said suddenly and sprang to his feet. "Well, it's not really it, but it's something!" For a man so large he moved remarkably quickly. The walls of his handsome room were lined with bookshelves. The back wall had wider shelves and contained an extraordinary melange of notebooks, files, folders, overflowing cardboard boxes, yellowing newspapers and old diaries. Into this chaos Mycroft plunged and began ferreting about at top speed.

"Mrs Hudson's always asking me if she can tidy this lot up, Inspector. I keep saying no because I'd never find anything again if she did. Is this it? No. How about you?" This question was addressed to an envelope that had once been white. "Yes? It is. Now then.

"This is the first thing that comes into my mind when you speak of bank notes and forgeries, Inspector. Here we have three brief newspaper accounts. Roach, aged thirty-two years, drowned in a sailing accident in the Lake District two years ago. The body was never found. Fettiplace-Jones, forty, fell out of a Channel ferry, remains never discovered, February last year. Browne, fifty, disappeared between his home in West Dulwich and the local railway station, never seen again, six months ago. Can you guess what all three had in common, Inspector? They all worked for Watermans, the Government printers. Watermans make all the currency notes for this country and most of the Empire too. All three were intimately involved in the design of bank notes and the machinery needed to produce them."

"God bless my soul," said Inspector Lestrade, watching as if hypnotised while Mycroft Holmes brushed another collection of white flakes of skin off his shoulder onto the floor.

"And there's worse to come, I fear, much worse." Holmes resumed his position, staring intently out of the window for a couple of minutes.

"You will remember, no doubt, Lestrade, the Napoleon of crime, Moriarty, Professor James Moriarty, who caused my brother such trouble and ended up at the bottom of the Reichenbach Falls. And then there was his confederate, Colonel Sebastian Moran, whose exploits and demise were described by the good doctor in The Adventure of the

Empty House? There is another such villain abroad today, a master of crime more evil and more sinister yet."

Mycroft Holmes paused again. "I fear we may be dealing with the Count!"

"The Count, Mr Holmes? Which Count?"

"Count or Graf von der Stoltenburg, Christian name Wolfgang and a wolf in wolf's clothing if ever there was one!"

"Has he been involved in forgery before?" asked Lestrade who had been taking notes of the various names as they came up.

"God knows what he has or has not been involved in. He was the brains behind the attempt to steal the Faberge Eggs and the Crown Jewels of the Tsar of all the Russias a few years back. I believe he was involved in the great swindle that caused the downfall of two leading finance houses in Frankfurt. He served in the German Army for some years with great distinction. He probably enjoyed killing people. When he left the Army he took a platoon load of men with him, engineers, linguists, street fighters of every description. All of them are now in his service, ready to return to the colours whenever he summons them. It is as though he is running a private army."

"Where would you like me to start?"

Mycroft looked at his watch. "I have to go to an emergency meeting about Dreadnoughts with the Chancellor of the Exchequer in ten minutes. Then I need to look at some papers in the Foreign Office and consult some of my opposite numbers in the Chancelleries of Europe. We are a small and secret band, we government auditors, but a group with much knowledge that is not in the public domain. One of my colleagues is in the habit of referring to it as The Underground Library. You must move fast, Lestrade. I suggest you go to the last known addresses of Roach, Fettiplace Jones and Browne. See what you can find. If they have been kidnapped or forced against their will to work on these forgeries their relatives may know if they are alive. The relatives will certainly deny it but their demeanour may tell you a different story. And the Count once had a London house, twenty-six Chester Square. Could you see if he is still there? He sometimes used his mother's maiden name rather than his own, Von Hoffmenstahl. I shall see you this evening at my club. I am always there from quarter to five to twenty to eight."

Holmes padded slowly down the stairs from his first-floor flat. Mrs Hudson was polishing the door knocker as he went past, oblivious to his housekeeper and his surroundings. He crossed the road and made his way to the Government offices. Over the years, as his importance grew, so did the size of his office in the Government Offices Great George Street. It was larger than that of the Chancellor of the Exchequer now, looking out over the inner courtyard. Mycroft had one of the largest desks in Europe at his command. It was over twelve feet long and was permanently covered in papers. It was the official equivalent of the back wall of his apartment. At the centre and at the two ends were bowls filled with Turkish Delight to oil the machinery of Mycroft's mind. He organised the dispatch of a long telegraph message to Germany. He wrote to the Minister of the Interior in Berlin, a key member of the Underground Library, called Tycho von Wilamowitz Mollendorff, who replied that as far as he knew, the Graf was not in Germany. Von Wilamowitz Mollendorff was, however, able to speak to the vast schloss in Silesia which served as the Hauptquartier or Headquarters of the Count's private army on the telephone. Mycroft remembered that von Stoltenburg owned over half the coal in Silesia. The Underground Library man in Berlin relayed the news that the Graf was away on business and nobody knew when he would return.

The third and final call, this time by telephone, was to Thierry Bastien-Tinville, a leading Paris banker. For once, the Frenchman had no fresh intelligence about the whereabouts of the Count. Sitting quietly in the corner of the office, reading some Government documents, was Mycroft's assistant, a young man called Tobias. In many ways he was the opposite of his master. Where Holmes was tall and corpulent, Tobias was short and pencil thin. While Mycroft's eyesight was still first class, Tobias peered at the world through thick glasses. Tobias was born into a family of schoolteachers in Shakespeare's home town of Stratford-upon- Avon. Most parents read bedtime stories to their children. Tobias' parents, Hilda and Arthur, read him the multiplication tables in a sing- song voice. The little boy would drift off to sleep to the musical lilt of seven sevens are forty-nine, seven eights are fifty-six. By the time he was six they had reached the twelve times table. They just kept going. At the age of twenty-one Tobias graduated as Senior Wrangler in Mathematics – top of his year – at Cambridge and went on to join Mycroft at the Government Auditor's office. There was only one passion in Tobias' life: Tottenham Hotspur Football Club. By the end of the season he could tell you every single result and who had scored the goals.

Mycroft had told the young man about the forgeries before he made his calls.

"Before we get down to business, sir," said Tobias, "there's one thing I think you should know about. It's odd, very odd."

"What's that?" said Mycroft, popping a Turkish Delight into his mouth.

"The crime figures are down, sir. In some parts of the country, London and Liverpool, for example, armed robbery has virtually disappeared. You'd think the police would be congratulating themselves about their success in lowering the crime rate, but they're keeping very quiet. They've hidden the figures away in the back of this report to the Home Secretary."

"They don't want anybody to know about it in case the politicians decide they need fewer policemen or less money from the Government, I expect. But it is, as you say, very odd. Now then, we need to turn our attention to these rumours about attempts to debase the currency." Mycroft leaned back in his chair and cupped his hands round the bottom of his stomach. "There are, I think, three questions we need to address. I think we have to work on the assumption that the rumours are correct and an attempt is being made to debase the currency. The first is this, and it is almost a metaphysical one. Does anybody know how many genuine banknotes there are in circulation? And how would you find out if that number has been exceeded by the activities of the forgers? The second is a question of location. To make the forgeries, the forgers must have a printing press or presses or, maybe, access to one owned by a government printer. Where would you put them? In England or on the Continent? And the third question is, in my judgement, the most difficult. How do you flood the country with fake money? The forgers could use it for their private purposes, they could buy property with it, they could take it to fashionable watering places and casinos, but that's not going to have much impact nationally, certainly not enough to debase the currency. I suggest that you start work on the first and the third question, Tobias. I don't have to tell you that you must be very careful when you speak to some of these people. The Treasury and the officials at the Bank of England can't discover what we are really about."

"I'll tell them I'm writing an article for an academic economic journal, sir," said Tobias cheerfully. "I've a friend who runs one of these things, full of obscure bits of theory. I'll tell them I'm looking at the circulation of money and the velocity it attains on its travels round the economy. I reckon I could lose them in the jargon inside five minutes."

"Good," said Mycroft. "I'm going to consult the last three annual reports from Watermans and the latest stuff from the Bank of England." Mycroft padded over to the left-hand wall and returned with a series of folders. He reflected that their ammunition might seem rather dry in the battle against the forgers but he had always been a great believer in the power of his brain and his own deductive abilities.

Diogenes the ancient philosopher lived at the same time as Plato and was famous, among other things, for walking about with a lit lamp in his hand in the daylight, looking, he said, for an honest man. Mycroft and his friends had founded the Diogenes Club because the philosopher was famous for his dislike of socialising and social life in general. The principal rule of the Club was that you could only speak in the Strangers Room. Silence was to be observed in the reading room, the bar, the dining room, the billiard room and the library. Anybody reported three times for speaking in the wrong place was automatically expelled by the committee. Entrance was conducted by means of a written test rather than an interview.

As Inspector Lestrade was shown into the Strangers Room, he caught a glimpse of the Reading Room where men were sitting by themselves reading the newspapers, or falling asleep in their armchairs. Mycroft appeared out of a door concealed in the bookcases at the far end of the room.

"Good Evening, Lestrade, I was looking something up in the archives down in the cellar," he said, showing the Inspector into a chair by the fire. "What do you have to report?"

"Well, Mr Holmes, I began with that house in Chester Square where you said the Count had lived a few years ago. It's been sold to an American gentleman, man by the name of Morgan. The butler said he thought the Count had gone to live in the country but he wasn't sure. Since then I've been on the trail of Roach, Fettiplace Jones and Browne all day. Two of them lived in Railway Cuttings in Slough, a neat row of cottages near the station. One of them, Mrs Roach, has moved to Hampstead, the other, Mrs Fettiplace Jones has apparently gone to live in Bray on the river. The estate agents have promised me the new addresses in the morning. But Mrs Browne is still there in a house on the outskirts of the town, not far from the Watermans manufactory."

"And what does she have to say for herself, Mrs Browne?"

"Well, you wouldn't say she was exactly prostrate with grief, Mr Holmes. It's six months now since her husband disappeared. There's a lot of new furniture about the house and some expensive looking silver. This is the curious thing, Mr Holmes. You know how difficult it is for the widows of people who disappear to claim any money from their insurance policies or pensions if they had any. It takes years and years before the authorities will pronounce them officially dead. When I asked Mrs Browne if she had started proceedings in this matter she admitted that she hadn't. She said she found it all too upsetting. She didn't look to me like the kind of woman who would find it too upsetting. I wouldn't be surprised if the husband were still alive, I really wouldn't."

"Have you talked to the Post Office?" asked Mycroft.

"Why should I talk to the Post Office, Mr Holmes? They aren't going to know where he is."

"You could be wrong there, my friend," said Mycroft. "They might know without knowing it, if you see what I mean."

"I don't, Mr Holmes, I don't see what you mean."

"It's quite simple, Lestrade. Let us assume that Browne has been kidnapped or hijacked, forced against his will to work for the forgers. He will want to let his wife know he is still alive. I doubt very much if the Count and his gang are in the habit of giving weekend passes to their victims. But they may let them write the occasional letter. Why don't you ask the Post Office to keep a record of all the postmarks on all the letters going to Mrs Browne and the other two? You're not allowed by law to open the letters and read them, but I'll have a word with the Home Secretary about that if we think we have discovered anything useful."

"I'll get onto it first thing in the morning, Mr Holmes. I should have thought of it myself."

"Never mind, Lestrade, you've done well finding them so fast. Continue your inquiries tomorrow. We can meet here at the same time." Mycroft paused suddenly and began to laugh. His stomach began to wobble with mirth.

"I've just thought of something, Lestrade. It's obvious when you think about it. The expensive silver, the furniture. If the Graf and his gang have got him, there's one thing the husband should have in abundance, certainly enough for a new sofa and a few pieces of plate. Maybe he's sending her regular supplies of money."

"What if he is, Mr Holmes, I don't understand."

"The money, Lestrade, the money. The man Browne is almost certainly keeping his wife afloat with regular supplies of banknotes. Forged banknotes. Forged banknotes that he has helped to create."

That evening Mycroft dined alone in a private room at the club. Not only was he a founder member of the Diogenes, but he chaired the catering committee and personally picked the chef. His brother Sherlock was an ascetic where food was concerned, never very interested in it, able to go for long periods without eating anything at all. Mycroft had the appetites, and enough hunger for the two of them. The chef, a Frenchman who learnt his trade in the hotels and restaurants of Lyon, had prepared for him that evening a fish soup of considerable subtlety and a steak with the chef's signature sauce. The porter brought him a letter and handed it over in silence. You had to write messages to the waiters in the Diogenes if you wanted more wine or an extra helping of the vegetables.

A note from Tobias was pinned on top of another note, written on HM Treasury notepaper. 'Sir,' Mycroft read, 'this from my friend who runs the economics journal.

"You ask about ways to flood the country with fake money and debase the currency. There are a number of ways of doing this. If you were the Bank of England you would circulate the money through the banks. If you owned a bank yourself you could keep issuing loans on the security of your forged notes and thus put the fake money into circulation. You could have loops of people endlessly changing large amounts of the fakes into German marks or French francs at the major banks or bureaux de change in all our large cities. But if, as I suspect, there is crime afoot here, the neatest way to flood the country with fake money would be to sell it to big criminal outfits. Five shillings for a five-pound note would seem a bargain to any criminal who can add up. The real criminals, the forgers, are invisible once the cash is handed over. The old fashioned criminals could then buy up assets like hotels or public houses with the phoney money and bank more than the takings to increase their wealth."

Hope this is useful. JMK.'

Mycroft made his way back to his rooms at his usual slow pace. The chef's own sauce, he reflected, had been a triumph and the sommelier's recommendation of a bottle of Romanee Conti to accompany the steak, a masterstroke. He would play a little on his baby grand piano when he reached home, he decided. His parents had been musical and very keen that both their sons should learn to play an instrument. They had played occasional duets, himself at the piano and Sherlock on his violin, and had once given an informal recital to family and friends at Christmas. Mycroft's mental powers were such that he could remember any piece perfectly after he had played it once. He now had a repertoire larger than most concert pianists. Mozart, he thought, as he dodged an enormous black car in the middle of Pall Mall. A Mozart piano concerto. That would be soothing for the nerves, for although his powers were as great as ever, their use at full stretch tired him out more and more as the years passed.

Early the following morning, Tobias had opened Mycroft's letters and a bundle of telegrams and laid them out on his desk. Even the act of opening an envelope was a tiresome bore for Mycroft and he would have left them lying about for weeks without his assistant. After a few moments he took a couple of telegrams and began walking up and down the room. This was so unusual that Tobias stared open mouthed as his master paraded around his vast office.

"Tobias," Mycroft said finally, returning to his desk and his chair and a generous helping of Turkish Delight, "this is progress. At last." He was still clutching his telegrams.

"These come from the firm in Germany that manufactures printing presses for most of the central banks of Europe. Some years ago they encountered a little financial difficulty. Their own government refused to help them. In desperation they turned to me by means of the Underground Library. I am glad to say that I was able to put together a series of measures which saw them through their troubles and which gave a very generous return over five years to the taxpayers of Great Britain. Yesterday I called in the debt. I asked for details of all the presses they had sold in the last five years. Normally this firm would not tell you the colour of their carpets or the names of their children. They are obsessed with secrecy. Each press is despatched in three different sections at different times. Each printing press is constructed in such a way that it will only work with the other two sections designed along with it. That, I may say, was one of my own suggestions all those years ago."

Mycroft smiled at the memory of his cleverness.

"They have answered all my inquiries. They have kept their side of the bargain, the Gesellschaft Franz Helmut Schinkler. In the last three years, apart from their contracts with their own government, they have sold printing presses for the manufacture of bank notes to Russia, Austria, Italy, Finland, Mexico and Andorra."

He paused. "Do you see the catch, Tobias?"

"I'm afraid I do not, sir. Not yet at any rate."

"Andorra does not have a currency of its own. They trade in French or Spanish money."

"But why should the German company manufacture a printing press for a country that didn't need one?"

"Here, my young friend, we see how clever the Count and his private regiment can be. Old man Schinkler tells me that they had a visitor who claimed to be a senior banker in the tiny country. Andorra, he told the Germans, was about to start printing its own currency. But they didn't want that known before they were ready. They had to have enough notes in hand to inject into the system before they announced the change. They had high hopes, the official from Andorra told the Schinkler people in confidence, that the notes would be popular with tourists and collectors, rather like rare stamps. Secrecy, the man said, was even more important than usual, so important that the Andorra Government were prepared to pay a twenty per cent premium on the price if the machinery reached Andorra without anybody finding out about it."

"And that was good enough for the Germans?"

"It was, Tobias, it was. And the premium has been paid. The good folk in Bavaria will think the launch has been postponed or the government has changed its mind. Somewhere out there, across the Channel or hidden away in this country is a printing press capable of producing enormous numbers of English banknotes. This is the first indication that the conspiracy really does exist."

Tobias was opening a note that had just been delivered. "This won't surprise you, sir. It's from the Treasurer of the Bank of England. He says they do not have an accurate idea of the exact number or the precise value of the notes in circulation. They have records of how many have been delivered by Watermans over the years, but they do not know how many have been lost or destroyed or buried under peoples' mattresses."

"That means," said Mycroft, "that we shall only know that the currency has been debased after it has happened and the price of everything has gone through the roof. There are certain indications already – they are very technical and will never be published – that prices are beginning to rise at a higher rate than normal."

Mycroft started shuffling the telegrams on his desk. In his mind's eye he could see his life's work auditing the Government departments, seeing off irregularities here, introducing superior methods there, destroyed by a fanatical

German count. Well, he would not go down without a fight. In one of his adventures with his brother, the affair of the Greek Interpreter, he had been persuaded to abandon his daily routine of Pall Mall, Department, Diogenes Club in the course of the inquiry. He had actually travelled to a different part of London. On another occasion he had been a cabbie, driving Dr Watson to a dangerous rendezvous with Sherlock Holmes at Victoria Station. These deviations from his routine had cost him dear. His nerves were shattered by the unaccustomed movement. He had been forced to take to his bed for ten days or more each time, and this before he had the services of Mrs Hudson to sustain him. Now, looking out at the fog that swirled round the inner courtyard of the Government Offices, Mycroft told himself that if he had to abandon his routine he would do so, whatever the consequences. It was the least he could do for his country.

"Tobias," he said, "I think we should go on the attack. Can you place the following advertisement in a prominent position in all the evening papers. 'Money for Sale. Five-pound Notes for Five Shillings. Anybody wishing to take advantage of this amazing offer should report to 68b Pall Mall at six o'clock tomorrow evening, Thursday. Deal closes at 7.30 pm'."

Tobias took the words down with his usual speed and headed for the private telegraph office next door, reserved exclusively by a grateful Government for the traffic of his master.

"What do you think may happen, sir," he asked as he reached the door.

"Well, nothing may happen," Mycroft replied. "People may think the offer is too good to be true. But consider,

Tobias. If your friend JMK is correct and this is how the money is distributed, the villains, the ordinary criminals, may think there is another goldmine opening up. They will not care how the money gets here, the criminals, they will just see an enormous profit. One or two of the villains may come along to check us out. There is another possibility, of course. The Count must have his people in London, maybe the infantry rather than the High Command, but representatives nonetheless. Surely they will see this advertisement or hear about it. They will wonder if they have competition. Who are these people offering money for nothing? Do we want them muscling in on our scheme? Lestrade must have men trailing every single person who comes to the rendezvous. And one other thing, Tobias. Can you talk to your contacts at the Bank of England? We'll need five thousand pounds in Treasury notes of every denomination in my rooms by five o'clock tomorrow afternoon."

"What should I say if they ask the reason, sir?"

"The reason? The reason? Ah yes, tell them it has to do with certain irregularities in the naval dockyards involved in Dreadnought construction. That could cover a multitude of sins. Indeed, now I think of it, it already does."

As Tobias set to work on the telegraph machines, Mycroft leant back in his chair, his mind darting out across England and the major powers on the Continent. Yesterday the plot had been insubstantial, shadowy. Now, with the revelations of the Andorra printing press, the enemy was coming into sight. And, with the advertisement in the evening papers, Mycroft felt he had issued a declaration of war.

Inspector Lestrade was in cheerful mood at the evening conference in the Strangers Room at the Diogenes Club. Mycroft was installed in a chair by the fire, smoking a brand of very strong cigarettes.

"Don't normally go in much for tobacco, myself. Little man in Jermyn Street runs these up for me, a thousand at a time. Virginia tobacco, extra strong."

Tobias was sitting quietly beside his master. Lestrade was waving the late edition of the evening paper in the air. Lestrade was not a man for the Oxford or Cambridge High Table or the more intellectual pursuits popular in the Athenaeum down the road. Action, that was what he liked, a few arrests, villains to interrogate, criminals to be charged and locked away.

"Would you like us to arrest them, Mr Holmes? Any people who turn up at your rooms in Pall Mall tomorrow?"

"Arrest them, Lestrade? Why ever should we arrest them? On what charges, pray?"

"Being in receipt of forged currency, of course," said the Inspector.

"But the notes will just have been delivered from the Bank of England itself!"

"They won't know that, will they? Even the most dim witted criminal from the East End will be able to work out that if you're selling a five pound note for five shillings, it must be a fake. Once we've got them all locked up we can see who will sing for their supper, or my name's not Lestrade!"

"My dear Lestrade," said Mycroft, taking a long pull at his cigarette, "your plan is admirable in its way, but there is one disadvantage. The criminal world will know at once that the scheme has the law behind it. They may suspend their operations which is the last thing we want. Follow them, follow them all, Lestrade. One or two may be known to your colleagues already and may be willing to talk, who knows. But we need to know who they are and where they come from. Unless I am very much mistaken, the Count and his people will want to have a look. They will want to see if they have competition on their hands. Do you see?"

"I do, Mr Holmes. You are playing a longer game than me. But what should I do if twenty people turn up? Or thirty? Or fifty?"

"My dear Lestrade, in that case you must have fifty officers lurking in the alleys round Pall Mall to follow all fifty if need be. This is a national emergency, not some break in down Bermondsey way."

"God bless my soul," said Inspector Lestrade, and helped himself to one of Mycroft's cigarettes.

Early the next morning it was the same routine as the day before. This was the shape of Mycroft's life. His apartment in Pall Mall. The Government Offices. The Diogenes Club. Another sheaf of papers, another bunch of telegraph messages, another Turkish Delight, another problem for the man who audited the accounts of all Government Departments. This morning he read three items of his correspondence twice and began writing furiously in a large red ledger in front of him. Normally, Mycroft did all his calculations up to the third decimal point in his head. Only arithmetic on a heroic scale needed to be written down. After three minutes hard work with his left hand there was a low sound, a sort of muted growl, as if an animal was in pain.

"This is bad, Tobias, very bad," he whispered.

"Sir?" said Tobias, looking up from his own paperwork.

"It's the prices. They're going up faster than we thought. The forgers are winning."

"How do you know that, sir?"

"Well, people often think prices are going up all the time. That's not quite true. Some prices go up, others come down. I have two means of my own for keeping track of price changes. I see the cost of all the raw materials for the Navy building their ships, timber, steel, guns, fittings of every sort."

Mycroft waved a bundle of papers in the air, as if they were to blame.

"Those costs are now going up at the rate of fifteen per cent a year. And I have a private arrangement with six leading shops and hotels in the capital here who send me figures every month for cost of raw materials, numbers of people employed, prices charged and profit earned. Those figures for the cost of raw materials are also going through the roof. This inflatiòn will soon be uncontrollable. We are losing the battle. We are in danger of going down to a heavy defeat."

"What can we do about it, sir?" asked Tobias, polishing his glasses with a fresh white handkerchief, washed and ironed by his mother.

"More than we are doing already, I mean."

There was a long pause. Mycroft flicked some more flakes off his shoulder with one hand and twirled his pen around with the other.

"I want you to set up a meeting for twelve o'clock this morning. The people invited will just have to drop whatever they are doing, Tobias. That milksop Governor of the Bank of England, I should never have sanctioned his appointment, he'd better come. Tell him to bring his expert on High Street banking with him, not one of their specialists in currency or international finance. And we want the Managing Director of Watermans and his expert on printing notes."

"Are you going to warn them about how serious the situation is, sir?

"More than that, Tobias, we need to have a set of arrangements in place to deal with the crisis."

"A sort of alternative plan, sir?"

"Exactly so, Tobias, exactly so."

Shortly after twelve o'clock the men were seated round the conference table at the far end of Mycroft's office. The Governor was looking worried, rubbing his hands together. The director of Watermans looked quite cheerful as if this meeting was preferable to whatever he had been doing before. The two experts were ready for action, pens and notebooks at the ready.

"Gentlemen," Mycroft began, "we are here to discuss a specific problem. For reasons of national security I cannot reveal the reasons behind this extraordinary gathering, but I trust you will believe me when I tell you that they are extremely serious. I want the answer to a simple question. How long would it take to change all of the nation's currency, not to get rid of the pound, but to replace all currency notes now in circulation with new ones to approximately the same value."

"God bless my soul," said the Governor. "That's a very difficult question. I would have to set up a special sub-committee at the Bank to consider the matter and get back to you."

Mycroft snorted and blew a mouthful of smoke in the general direction of the Governor.

"I presume, from what you say," said the printing expert from Watermans, a man in his early thirties with curly brown hair and the most expensive suit in the room called William Hooper, "that you would be wanting the design on the new notes to be noticeably different from the designs now in circulation?"

"You would be correct in that assumption, Mr Hooper," Mycroft replied, staring hard at the young man. Tobias, taking notes at the back of the room, had not expected that anybody would work out why the new currency was needed as fast as this.

"And would you want to replace them all at once, Mr Auditor? Or are there some that do not need replacing?"

"We need to replace them all. If we can do it in one go, that would be preferable."

William Hooper was scribbling furiously. "It's a pity we have lost so many of our key players in the last couple of years," he said. "Roach, Fettiplace-Jones, Browne, they have all been replaced, but the new men are not that experienced. If we just change the typefaces, that should take the least time. If we work twenty-four hours a day for the duration we could replace the designs in five weeks, a week for each note. Then it would take five days to print them with all the usual security measures. We would propose, in these unusual conditions, to produce the notes in six weeks. Please do not assume that we will be able to meet that target, but we will do our damnedest."

Tobias was wondering if Hooper had made the connection between forged notes in circulation and the disappearance of three of Watermans staff. He rather hoped not.

"I am much obliged to you, Mr Hooper," said Mycroft. "How long would it take to deliver the new notes, to put them in circulation, Mr Governor?"

The Governor mumbled into his beard. Mycroft shot another blast of smoke at him.

"If I might speak to that question, Mr Auditor," the Bank of England's High Street banking expert, Hugo Thomas, a tall thin man with greying hair, a small moustache and an MCC tie, "the key to the timescale is the distribution of the money all round the country. The plan would work like this. It would start on a fixed day, outside the holiday season, the first of October, the first of January, that sort of thing. On that day all the new notes would be introduced through the banks and finance houses and the big shops and would be legal tender. The old notes would continue to be valid for two months. At the end of that period the old notes would cease to be legal tender. So the whole process, taking into account the Waterman timetable, and allowing us two weeks to deliver the money round the country, the whole process could be completed in four months."

"Could we save a week or so if we used the Army to deliver the new currency?"

"We could, Mr Auditor, that is a helpful suggestion."

"Gentlemen," said Mycroft, "let me sum up for the Government. I want Mr Hooper and Mr Thomas to leave this meeting and draw up detailed plans for carrying out these proposals. I do not want them implemented yet, but I want them ready to move into action when I give the word. Thank you all very much for your time."

When the four visitors had left Mycroft kicked the leg of his desk in disgust.

"Four months!" he said. "Four bloody months! I didn't think it would take that long. In four months time prices could have gone through the roof and the British economy could be drifting towards the rocks."

Tobias had only seen Mycroft this angry once before when he had a life and death struggle with an incompetent Chancellor of the Exchequer who wanted to announce the abolition of income tax just before a general election.

"Perhaps we'll find out something to our advantage this evening when out visitors come to 68b, sir."

Mycroft cheered up. "The visitors, yes, the visitors. I had almost forgotten about our late afternoon guests."

Mrs Hudson made a special effort to clean up Mycroft's rooms while he was at his office that morning. Something in his manner when he told her he was expecting visitors at six o'clock led her to believe that one or two of them might be rather unorthodox citizens. She was well used to these kinds of gentlemen, having received all sorts and conditions of men from the King of Bohemia to Professor Moriarty himself in 221b Baker Street.

By a quarter to six that afternoon Mycroft's forces were in position. Seated at the little coffee table was Tobias, a fresh ledger in front of him. Lodged on the table was an open suitcase filled to the brim with Treasury notes of all denominations. Tobias's job was to receive and hand over the money. His boss felt that such exchanges were beneath the dignity of the Government Auditor. Mycroft was in his usual chair near the window. Seated on his left hand was a tall, burly man with a very large jacket with very large pockets and a pistol concealed in each one. This was Detective Sergeant Patrick Baldwin, one-time boxing champion of the Metropolitan Police, and in Inspector Lestrade's words, 'a good man in a rough house.'

Lestrade himself and another heavyweight policeman, this one a veteran of the second row of the Police Rugby Fifteen, were waiting in reserve in the spare bedroom. Lestrade had declared that they must be ready for all eventualities. Fifty more plain-clothes officers were deployed along Pall Mall. When a visitor left he would be followed.

The officers who began furthest away from 68B would gradually come closer as their colleagues set off on their missions of pursuit.

At one minute past six, there was a ring of the doorbell. Two lots of footsteps could be heard coming up the stairs. Detective Sergeant Baldwin put a hand in his pocket. Tobias fiddled with his tie. Lestrade was peering through the keyhole. Mycroft was smoking one of his foul cigarettes.

"A gentleman to see you, sir. Mr Smith."

Mycroft showed his visitor to a chair. The man was about forty years old and there was nothing remarkable about him at all. You would not have looked at him twice if you passed him in the street or sat next to him on the bus. He was an average man, average height, average amount of hair, a bland countenance. He looked round the room, the portly figure of Mycroft, the tall plain-clothes policeman, Tobias and the money. His gaze locked onto the suitcase full of notes.

"I have come about the money," he began.

"Indeed so, Mr Smith," said Mycroft.

"Would you permit me to examine one of the five-pound notes? I shall do no business here without an examination."

"Is it only the five-pound notes you are interested in, Mr Smith?"

"That is correct."

Tobias handed him a crisp new five-pound note. The man held it up to the light. He ran his right hand very slowly over the surface. When he put his other hand in his pocket Detective Sergeant Baldwin tightened his grip on his pistol.

Smith brought out a magnifying glass of considerable power. He examined the note for another couple of minutes.

"It's a very fine piece of work," he said. "One of the best I've seen."

"Do you see many forgeries, Mr Smith?" said Mycroft.

"I've seen a lot in my time, sir."

"Recently?" asked Mycroft.

"That's as maybe. I haven't come here to discuss recent forgeries. I'll take fifty pounds worth of these five pound notes if I may."

"Do you mean you will give me fifty pounds of your pounds, or do you want fifty pounds of my pounds?"

Tobias had worked out that if Smith handed over fifty pounds, he, Tobias, would have to hand over one thousand. A fifth of his capital would be gone inside five minutes.

"I will give you fifty of these pounds, Mr Holmes. In return, as per your advertisement, I expect one thousand of your notes on that table." Smith had put his hand into the breast pocket of his jacket and laid down fifty pounds in five rather battered ten-pound notes on the coffee table. Tobias handed over a thousand pounds worth of five-pound notes in bundles of a hundred at a time. Smith checked that there were genuine notes and not blank pieces of paper in each pile. He stowed the money in various pockets and stood up.

"Thank you gentlemen," he said, "and a very good afternoon to you all." The transaction had taken less than ten minutes.

Five minutes passed, then ten. Tobias was beginning to wonder if they would only have one customer. At twenty past six there was another ring at the front door bell.

"A gentleman to see you, sir. Mr Hammond."

Mycroft knew Hammond by sight. He kept the greengrocer's shop not far from his offices.

"Mr Holmes, it is you," said the greengrocer who was still wearing his work uniform of brown apron with a tattered cap that had once been blue on his head. "It must be alright then."

"Good to see you, Hammond. Have you come to buy some money?"

"That's what I meant just now when I said it must be alright, sir. It's my little boy, Mr Holmes," the greengrocer went on, "he's very sick and they say he needs all kinds of treatment I can't afford. Not the way things are at the moment, if you understand me."

Hammond was twisting his hands together as he spoke. "I've only got five pounds," he went on, "that's all I have managed to save these last five years, four children being so expensive to bring up."

"My dear Hammond," Holmes handed a rather grubby five pound note over to Tobias who placed it carefully in an envelope and wrote Second Man on it in large letters, "you did well to come here to us today. For reasons I cannot explain this offer ends in another an hour and ten minutes time. How would you like the money?" Tobias had noted before how Mycroft seemed to have a clock in his brain which told him the precise time of day whenever he wanted to know it, without needing to glance at a watch or a clock.

"Five-pound notes would be best," said Hammond. Tobias handed over twenty brand new notes. "Do you know, Mr Holmes," said the greengrocer, staring in wonder at his new wealth, "I've never had this much money in my hand, not once. I'm so grateful."

With that the greengrocer hurried towards the door. "Just one last thing, Mr Holmes," he said, "there's nothing funny about these notes, is there? They're not fake, are they?"

"They're fine," said Mycroft with a smile. "You could take them down to the Bank of England right now, and they'd tell you they're absolutely genuine."

"I didn't think there'd be anything funny going on with you involved, Mr Holmes. I'm so grateful. Good evening to you both."

As the door closed behind him Mycroft rose to his feet and took up a position by the window. As the greengrocer passed up the street, a slim figure in a battered raincoat detached itself from a doorway and followed him towards Whitehall. But it was another figure that held Mycroft's attention, a small man lurking behind a pillar by the entrance to The Hypocrites Club across the road. He slipped onto the pavement while a bus was passing. Two minutes later he was shown into the room by Mrs Hudson.

"Mr Jones, sir," she announced. Mycroft doubted very much if he was inspecting a genuine Jones as the man sat down. Names in this case, he reflected, were as fickle as forgeries. The man was in his middle thirties, of average height, clean-shaven with large eyes that seemed to flicker between grey and a light blue. He was wearing heavy boots not often seen in London's West End. He had a long scar running down his right cheek.

"These notes of yours," Jones began, "I would like to inspect some if I might be allowed."

He spoke with a very slight accent, as if English might not be his mother tongue, or he had lived abroad for a long time. Like the first caller, Mr Smith, he took a note out of his own pocket and compared it with the five-pound note handed over by Tobias. Then he held them up to the light. Out came the microscope. Jones turned the two notes over and over until his eyes must have grown tired of looking at them. He ran a finger very gently down his cheek with the scar.

"Thank you, gentlemen," he said, returning the note to Tobias. "I have a proposition to put to you. I am here as the representative of a group, a consortium, of investors. They are very interested in your notes. That is why they sent me here to investigate them. I have made a preliminary inspection. I would like to take two representatives of each denomination away with me to make further tests. I shall, of course, pay for them. If I and my colleagues are satisfied with the notes, we would like to purchase whatever number you have currently available, and commission more if you have the ability to produce them. Would this plan be agreeable?"

"Of course," said Mycroft. "We have a fraction under four thousand pounds to hand at present. More can be produced later, of course. But I am anxious not to be left in possession of all this cash for too long, Mr Jones. When do you intend to return?"

"Between eight and nine tomorrow morning, sir, if that would be in order?"

"Capital," said Holmes. "I look forward to seeing you then." Jones and Tobias exchanged notes. Jones bowed slightly as he left the room.

"Good evening, gentlemen."

Once more Mycroft sidled over to the window. Two men seemed to appear as if from nowhere and slipped into the rush hour crowd bearing Jones out towards Lower Regent Street and the Haymarket.

"Well, Mr Holmes," said Lestrade, exploding out the spare bedroom like a bullet from a gun, "what did you make of our friends?"

"You couldn't see very much, of course, Inspector, but I would suggest you endeavour to make less noise when you kneel down to look through a keyhole in future. I could hear your every move quite distinctly."

"Sorry about that, Mr Holmes," said the man from Scotland Yard. "But what did you make of them?"

"The shoes were interesting, very interesting," said Mycroft, rising once more to peer out into Pall Mall. "We have had rain today. The first and the second man just had damp marks on the bottom of their shoes. But the third man had traces of country mud on those great boots of his, mud that you would not find within five miles of Hyde Park Corner unless you were stomping about in one of the parks. Jones, the third man, has come in from the country. We will have to wait for the reports from your officers a little later before we know their addresses. I suggest you go and wait for that information,

Lestrade. And Tobias, you must take yourself to the Bank of England with the money our friends handed over. Their expert with the machine that can detect the forgeries will be waiting. I suggest we meet again at my club at nine thirty. There should be news by then."

Lestrade hurried off. Tobias put the three envelopes in an inside pocket. "Do you think any of the money those people handed over will be fake, sir?"

"Do you want my honest opinion, Tobias? I think at least one will be a forgery. One, if not two."

At nine thirty that evening Mycroft was still waiting for the return of Lestrade and Tobias. He was sipping a large glass of Armagnac and trying to put himself in the position of the forgers. Would they have made England or some Continental country the base for their operations? A city? A town? A grand house in the middle of nowhere? He was weighing up the possibilities of a remote corner of Spain when Lestrade rushed in, panting and looking distraught.

"I'm so sorry, Mr Holmes," he gasped, "we've lost one of them. Lost him completely."

"Which one?"

"The third one, Jones he called himself, the man with the scar. He walked into the central section of Paddington

Station and seemed to disappear. If he got on a train then my men didn't spot him, or where the train was going to. I've sent word to the main stations out of Paddington but I'm not hopeful."

"What happened to the other two?"

"The first man, the one who called himself Smith, lives in Hammersmith. Nice house, apparently. One of my men will go back tomorrow to get the details of his employment and so on. Your greengrocer lives on one floor of a small house in Hackney. A man presumed to be a doctor was seen leaving the place by a neighbour shortly before our officer arrived."

Tobias, grinning happily, slipped into the room and helped himself to a small glass of Armagnac.

"It's exactly like you said, sir," he said, addressing himself to Mycroft, "two of the notes were forgeries. Your greengrocer's note was so battered the expert wasn't sure – he didn't think his machine would work properly on it – but he gave it a clean bill of health in the end."

"Think of it," said Lestrade, "two out of three of them forgeries! Who would have thought it?"

"Well," said Mycroft, "the advertisement was something like a trap. It shows we have to redouble our efforts. I have been trying to put myself in the position of the Count and his forgers. I will give you the results of my thinking in the morning. Tobias, could you summon the heads of the three leading estate agents in London and the Home County to my office tomorrow morning? Shall we say eleven o'clock? And Lestrade, can you warn your superiors that we may require a large body of men at any time in the next week. Not your cleverest, or your most efficient, but fit men who can run fast and look after themselves."

Mycroft Holmes did not go to bed that night. Like his brother he had the capacity for long periods of strenuous mental activity on very little sleep. He did, however require regular helpings of food. Mrs Hudson left him two plates of sandwiches and an entire chocolate cake to fuel his thoughts through the hours of darkness. He smoked a lot that night and failed to open any windows so that his room resembled one of London's thicker fogs by the morning. He would stare out of his window for periods of half an hour or more at a stretch, his brain not taking in the stray dogs and stray people on patrol in Pall Mall in the night hours. Shortly after three o'clock he was looking out of his window at the gas lamp opposite. Something moved. The profile was one he knew well. It could not be! His brother Sherlock was surely asleep in his bed in Sussex, not prowling the night streets of London! There it was again, that familiar profile, slipping away! Had it been looking up at his windows? When he rubbed the windowpane to get a better view, the phantasm had vanished. Pall Mall, as far as Mycroft could see, was totally deserted.

Mrs Hudson threw open the windows when she brought him his breakfast at precisely seven thirty. Just after eight o'clock she was back.

"This gentleman demands to see you at once, sir. He would not be put off even though it is so early. He has not given me a name."

"Don't worry, Mrs Hudson," said Mycroft, waving his guest to a chair. The visitor was over six feet tall with a small grey moustache. His hair was swept back and heavily oiled. The most remarkable thing about him was his eyes. They glittered. Looking at them Mycroft thought the man had the eyes of a fanatic. He carried a stout walking stick in his right hand.

"Please let me introduce myself. Graf von Stoltenburg at your service, Mr Holmes."

"Good morning to you, Graf," said Mycroft, shovelling a large amount of lime marmalade on to the last piece of toast. He had a carried a violent dislike of orange marmalade since he had to endure the stuff they served up at his boarding school.

"Please do not interrupt me further while I am speaking to you, Mr Holmes. I shall not detain you long. I have come here this morning to warn you. Your activities are beginning to displease me. I know all about your meetings with bankers and your queries about my presence in my native country. Your activities will cease immediately. If they do not, your life will become very different and rather painful. In my business, minor foes, Mr Holmes, are shot at once. More serious enemies take longer to die in my custody."

He flicked a switch at the top of his walking stick and drew out a long thin sword. He prodded Mycroft in the stomach.

"Perhaps it will be time to lose a little weight, no? Perhaps we will flay the skin off your bones like Marsyas in the fable. Maybe we will have you dance to the electric current. Maybe all three at the same time. People have often praised me for the originality of my schemes for making money and damaging society. I am equally original in devising the means and methods of death. You have been warned, Mr Holmes. Cease your activities and live. Continue and you will die. A very good morning to you."

Mycroft looked into those fanatic eyes. "Good morning to you too, Graf. Please remember to close the door on your way out."

So very German, he said to himself as the Prussian boots echoed down the stairs. There were exceptions, of course, Bach, Beethoven, Goethe and a few more. But on the whole he thought the Graf was like the majority of his fellow countrymen, unspeakably vulgar.

Mrs Hudson had been listening at the door. When the Count had gone she sent word to Lestrade that Mr Holmes's life was in great danger. The graph, she wrote, remembering her mathematics lessons at school, was threatening to kill him.

At eight thirty precisely the man with the scar was back. Tobias was already in position with the money. The man handed over two hundred pounds in ten-pound notes. He received the entire suitcase and departed, merely observing that he would be in touch presently to commission some more notes.

When Mycroft set off for his office at eight forty five, he was followed by four plain-clothes detectives, and Inspector Lestrade was waiting for him in his office.

"Pshaw, man, pshaw!" said Mycroft when informed of the plain-clothes men watching out for his life. "Let the Count try what he will. Quite soon, I hope, the affair will be over."

"I am astonished you should say that, Mr Holmes." Inspector Lestrade looked confused. "Why, you haven't gone anywhere or even been to see the quarters of the men who bought the forged money."

"You must not expect me to behave like my brother, Inspector," said Mycroft, popping a Turkish Delight into his mouth. "Sherlock was forever running about, crawling along the ground if he felt the need to look for footprints in the snow or scraps of a lady's dress that had been torn in some domestic conflict. That is not my way."

He paused to make a note in his black notebook. "You could say that my brother built up his cases based on the facts. He was always keen on what he referred to as the facts. The visitors to his consulting rooms in Baker Street were seldom asked to do anything other than relate the facts of the case. Out of all this information and what he discovered in his researches at locations like the stables with the missing Silver Blaze he assembled his evidence to reveal the truth. My own method is rather different. I try to deduce the circumstances of the case to fit whatever we know. Once we know that the disagreeable Graf von Stoltenburg is at the centre of the case, we know we have a worthy opponent and a mighty crime to hand in all these forgeries. During yesterday and last night I formed a working hypothesis about this business. Quite soon I hope that we can try it out."

Mycroft ambled over to his window and looked out at Horse Guards Parade. Both Lestrade and Tobias expected him to flesh out his theory, to tell them what his hypothesis was. But he did not speak another word and returned to continue writing notes at his desk.

The representatives of London's three leading estate agents arrived promptly at eleven o'clock. They looked rather similar, all clean-shaven, all wearing dark blue suits with white shirts and gold cuff links. One was bald. One had a slight limp from a hunting accident. One was fiddling with a silver fountain pen in his left hand.

"Good morning, gentlemen," said Mycroft. "Thank you for coming so promptly. We are in need of your expertise and we need it very quickly."

"How can we help, Mr Holmes," said the bald estate agent who appeared to be the spokesman.

"We are looking for a country house within a thirty to forty mile radius of London. I fancy it is most likely to be to the West, within easy reach of London and the main line to Bristol and Exeter. It will have extensive grounds, well set back from the public view and the public road. I imagine there will be a gatehouse or two round the edge."

The estate agents were all writing furiously. Lestrade was staring at Mycroft as if he had just dropped down from a distant planet.

"One of the key things about this house should be its basement. This will be large with very strong floors. It may have been extended recently. The house will be furnished with electric light and the telephone equipment. I fancy there will be an instrument in the main gatehouse as well. The house will have been bought by its current owner sometime in the last eighteen months, probably less than that. It might have found its way onto the pages of Country Life. It is, I fear, rather a Country Life sort of house."

The three estate agents stared at Mycroft. Then the bald one spoke once more. "Very good, Mr Holmes. We shall set to work right away." Mycroft shook each man by the hand as they left. Lestrade was still looking astounded.

"How on earth, Mr Holmes," he began.

"Let us not waste time on trifles, my dear Inspector. Just consider the evidence. You lost the man at Paddington station, the gateway to the West of England. He had mud on his boots. Printing presses are very heavy. Men attempting to debase the currency are not likely to go about their work on the main road where anybody might see them. And the fact that Graf von Stoltenburg is in London leads me to think that the centre of operation must be here in England rather than on the Continent."

Mycroft walked slowly to his window. "One of your men is coming in a great hurry, Inspector, and from the look on his face I should say he is the bearer of bad news."

Seconds later there was a loud thump of boots and a knock on the door. A rather flustered plain-clothes man rushed in.

"He's done it again, sir, he's done it again!"

"Who has done what, Johnston, stop speaking in riddles."

"Sorry, sir, it's the man with the scar, sir. We had two men waiting to follow him. He was wearing a beige raincoat and a trilby hat, sir. By the end of Pall Mall there were two men in beige raincoats with trilby hats. By Lower Regent Street there were four. Then one turned off into Piccadilly, one went up Regent Street and the other two headed off in the direction of the Haymarket and Leicester Square, sir. Our men were so confused they lost all confidence in their abilities and retired to have a cup of tea, I'm afraid to say. They were quite shaken up by the one man turning into four."

"Damn, damn and damn again!" said Lestrade, walking rapidly round the room. "We've been humbugged again. You said this Graf whatever his name is, must be a clever villain,

Mr Holmes. That was certainly pretty sharp work this morning."

Salvation came in the afternoon. It came in the form of a letter, typed at great speed and with a number of errors, addressed to Mycroft.

'The house we want,' it said, 'is called The Silver Birches, near Reading. It sits one mile to the left on the road from Pangbourne to Tidmarsh, on the left hand side with a pair of gate lodges and a couple of dirty white pillars. Recent sign talks of guard dogs on patrol. House six hundred yards up the drive. Lestrade.'

"Well, Tobias," said Mycroft, handing him the note, "there we are. A house near the Thames." He wondered if he should go in person. He reminded himself that only the other day he had promised himself that if duty and his country called, he would leave his office, his club and his rooms, whatever the cost. He was still considering the matter when the telephone rang. Tobias answered it. Mycroft Holmes was not in the habit of answering the telephone.

"It's for you, sir,"

Mycroft picked up the telephone and examined it carefully.

"Yes, sir," he said a number of times. Mycroft knew the voice well. How many times had he sat in on Cabinet meetings as auditor of all Government Departments and heard that voice sum up the arguments and pronounce on policy. The voice was always measured but carried the authority of years in the most important office in Great Britain.

"Of course, sir," said Mycroft as he put the phone down. "Tobias, that was the Prime Minister. He wants me, as he put it, to be in on the kill in this business. There may be some eventualities the police would not be capable of solving. The train for Pangbourne leaves from Paddington, if I am not mistaken, and takes forty-two minutes to reach its destination."

Inspector Lestrade was waiting by the gate lodge, a stout stick in his right hand. "Glad you could make it, Mr Holmes. We've only just got here ourselves. Most of my men are waiting round the next bend. A small party has gone to reconnoitre the main house. I've got forty officers in total. That should be enough. I'm going to put a couple of rings of men round the house. When they're in place, the rest of us will storm in. There's an old lady in there," he nodded to the gate lodge on the right, "who's got the keys. She's got a bundle of about twenty-five on one ring."

Fifteen minutes later Lestrade departed for a conference with his advance guard. Mycroft Holmes was shivering slightly. He was feeling unwell already. The sickness had started in the train. He wondered how much worse it was going to get. Tobias was looking at him anxiously.

"Right then, Mr Holmes," Lestrade was back, rejoicing in the prospect of action and, possibly, a fight. "I've got my orders, Mr Holmes, from the Commissioner himself, no less. You're to stay behind here in the lodge. The Government cannot have their finest auditor run the risk of a stray bullet from a Prussian pistol. You're much too valuable to be involved in any action, that's what my Commissioner says."

Lestrade looked closely at Tobias, the thin frame, the thick glasses, the faint air Tobias always carried with him of being the classroom swot. He decided that Tobias wouldn't be much use either if it turned rough, "You'd better stay with Mr Holmes, young Tobias. We may need you to run messages later on."

Inspector Lestrade knocked on the door and summoned the crone. She looked well over seventy years old. She was wearing a long woollen dress that might once have been grey and a vast collection of scarves in different colours. She was bent over like a human question mark, and held her bundle of keys firmly in her left hand. Mycroft stared at the crone's hands. There was something about them with their long thin fingers that seemed to remind him of something, something to do with his childhood long ago. He shook himself suddenly. The illness must be worse than he thought. It was playing tricks with his mind. He would have to go directly to bed when re reached home. Mrs Hudson could bring him some of her excellent beef tea.

"Could you take us to the house now, please," said the Inspector. The crone nodded and shuffled slowly up the drive. Lestrade followed, his men falling in behind. The old lady was muttering to herself, pointing at the police officers.

"Five, six, seven."

Lestrade stared at her.

"Nine, ten, eleven…"

It took him some tine to realise that the old lady was counting the number of policemen.

"Tobias," said Mycroft, "did you remember to bring any Turkish Delights with you?

"I did, sir."

"Thank you so much," said Mycroft, helping himself to two at the same time, "I have to tell you that I am feeling more unsettled and ill with every minute that passes. I fear that I shall be confined to bed with the Consolidated Treasury Accounts and the Customs and Excise Depositions for days, if not weeks, on our return. However, I feel we should interpose ourselves on the action closer to the house. We shall hear news quicker that way. Come, Tobias. Let us advance upon the finale."

One slim and young, one stout and old figure moved slowly up the drive towards the house. One hundred yards from the gate lodge Mycroft stopped suddenly and stared at Tobias.

"Of course, of course," he said quietly, as if speaking to himself. "It all fits in. How stupid of me not to see it before. You remember telling me at the beginning of the investigation, Tobias, that the figures for armed robbery had dropped all over the country?"

"I do, sir," said Tobias, wondering if the changed routine was affecting his master's wits.

"It's perfectly obvious once you know what we know now. The criminals don't need to rob any more. They've got, or bought, however they managed it, more money from the Count and his forgeries than they could have ever obtained from robbing banks and breaking into people's houses to steal their valuables. Speaking in my role as Auditor of all Government Departments I still think it is a bad bargain. A stable currency is more useful to a country than a falling crime rate, however welcome that might be in the short term. Goodness me, the villains must have thought every day was Christmas!"

Mycroft and Tobias set off again. They could see a great sentry guard of silver birch trees all around the house. Soon they heard great shoutings and whistlings. As Mycroft and Tobias grew close to the main entrance, they saw a number of men being handcuffed and thrown into the police vehicles that would lead them to the cells of London.

"Mr Holmes," said Lestrade, panting after his exertions, "congratulations on finding the house! A masterstroke! It has been a triumph for your detecting skills! How I prefer action to speculation! At last! They were outnumbered, my friend. Our forces entered the basement from three different doors, opened for us by the old lady with the scarves. Four criminals were apprehended supervising the workings of the great printing press, turning out ten-pound notes at incredible speed. Two of them were the people who had vanished earlier, Roach and Fettiplace Jones. Others were packing the notes into cardboard boxes. We have arrested the lot!"

"But what of the Graf, Lestrade?" said Mycroft, "Has he been apprehended?"

"Roach said he was there, Mr Holmes. But we have found nobody matching the description you gave us."

"Has he got away? Has the house a tunnel, Lestrade? Many of these places have underground passages linking the stable block with the kitchens in the basement so that goods could be brought into the house without the owners seeing what was going on. God help England if Graf von Stoltenburg has got away!"

"I shall send men to find out, Mr Holmes!" Lestrade paused to issue instructions to a couple of his officers.

"But tell me, Mr Holmes, how did you find out about the location of this house?"

"Why, Lestrade, you sent me a note. I have it in my pocket. Let me ask you, pray, how you found about it?"

"Why, you sent me a note about it, Mr Holmes."

"I did not send you a note, Lestrade. Certainly not. Do you have it on your person?"

Lestrade fiddled about it his pockets. "There we are, Mr Holmes. That is the note you sent me."

Mycroft snorted. "I did not send this. You did not send a message to me. I do not do the typing on these ridiculous machines. Tobias does all that for me. Both notes were written on the same typewriting machine, with a damaged capital 'r', a 'k' with one leg missing and an irregular return on the space bar. There is only one possible explanation!"

Tobias had wandered off, away from the house, and returned with a bundle of crumpled clothes.

"Forgive me," he said, "but surely these are the woollen dress and the innumerable scarves, worn by the old crone who took you to the house? And look!"

Tobias pointed dramatically towards the little hill that lay between the house and the river. A tall, slim figure was standing at the highest point. A thick blast of pipe smoke arose to meet the early evening mist that rose from the river at this time. The figure performed an elaborate bow.

"Holmes?" said Inspector Lestrade. "Holmes?"

"Holmes?" said Mycroft, smiling at the memory of the old crone's hands that had also been his brother's hands which had worked the violin when they combined in their music duets all those years before, "Sherlock Holmes! It must have been he who found the house! Elementary, my dear Lestrade, elementary!"

Also in *The Mycroft Holmes series:*

Mycroft Holmes and The Adventure of the Silver Birches
Mycroft Holmes and The Adventure of the Naval Engineer
Mycroft Holmes and The Case of the Missing Popes
Mycroft Holmes and The Bankers' Conclave
Mycroft Holmes and Murder at the Diogenes Club
Mycroft Holmes: The Case of the Romanovs Pearls

*

Printed in Great Britain
by Amazon